For Carol
P. R.

For little Sophie,
my great-niece,
with love
H.C.

First published 1996 by Walker Books Ltd
87 Vauxhall Walk, London SE11 5HJ

2 4 6 8 10 9 7 5 3 1

Printed in Hong Kong

This book has been typeset in Calligraphic Antique.

British Library Cataloguing in Publication Data
A catalogue record for this title is available
from the British Library.

ISBN 0-7445-4073-9

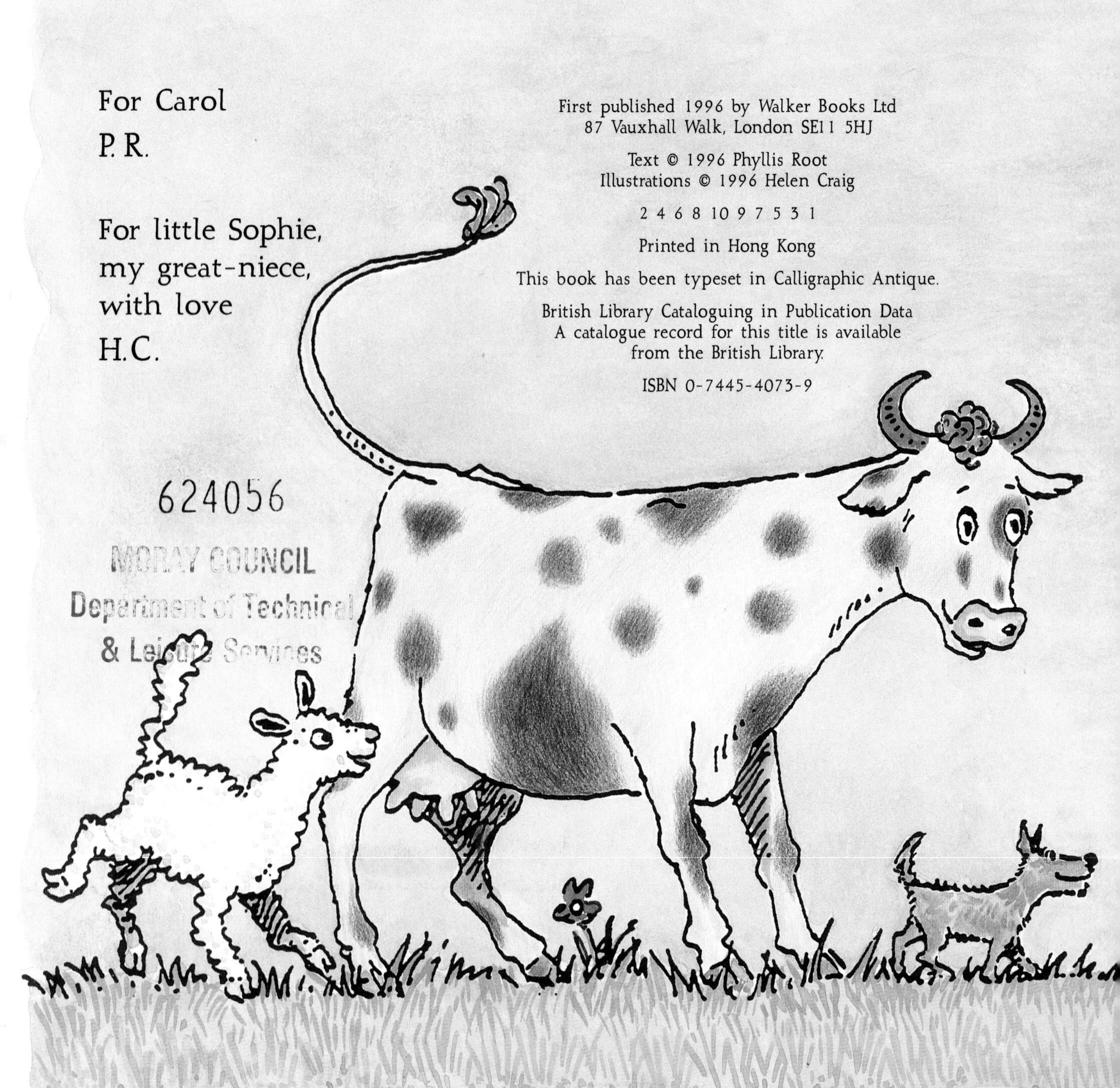

One Windy Wednesday

Written by
PHYLLIS ROOT

Illustrated by
HELEN CRAIG

WALKER BOOKS
AND SUBSIDIARIES
LONDON • BOSTON • SYDNEY

One Wednesday, Bonnie Bumble felt the wind begin to blow.

It blew
and it blew
and it blew.

It blew the
quack right out
of the duck.

It blew the moo
right out of
the cow.

It blew the
oink right out
of the pig.

It blew the baa
right out of
the lamb.

"Moo!" said the duck.

"Oink!" said the cow.
OINK!

"Quack!" said the lamb.
QUACK!

"Baa!" said the pig.

"What a mess!" said Bonnie Bumble.

When the wind died down
she worked to put everything right.

She patted the
quack back on
to the duck.

She hitched
the moo back
on to the cow.

She tied the oink back
on to the pig.

She knitted the baa
back on to the lamb.

"Moo!"
said the cow.

"Quack!"
said the duck.

"Oink!"
said the pig.

"Baa!"
said the lamb.

"That's better," said
Bonnie Bumble,
all worn out.

Just then a little breeze blew by.
"Meow, meow, meow,"
said the dog!

MEOW!